Mulan and the Dragon Race

By Kathy McCullough
Illustrated by the Disney Storybook Art Team

A Random House PICTUREBACK® Book

Random House 🏠 New York

Copyright © 2020 Disney Enterprises, Inc. All rights reserved. Published in the United States by Random House Children's Books, an imprint of Penguin Random House LLC, 1745 Broadway, New York, NY 10019, and in Canada by Penguin Random House Canada Limited, Toronto, in conjunction with Disney Enterprises, Inc. Pictureback, Random House, and the Random House colophon are registered trademarks of Penguin Random House LLC.
rhcbooks.com
ISBN 978-0-7364-4120-9
Printed in the United States of America
10 9 8 7 6 5 4 3 2

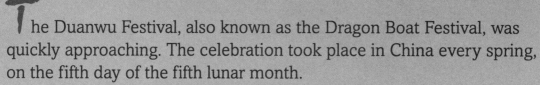

The Duanwu Festival, also known as the Dragon Boat Festival, was quickly approaching. The celebration took place in China every spring, on the fifth day of the fifth lunar month.

Mulan's favorite part was the Dragon Boat Race. Each year, Mulan watched the boats from other villages race down the river.

This year, Mulan wanted to do more than watch.

"Our village should enter the race!" Mulan told her family. Her father agreed that it would bring honor to their village. But her mother was worried. The village had never taken part in the race before.

"There's a first time for everything," Grandma Fa reminded her.

When Mulan announced her idea, the villagers were hesitant.

Mulan recalled Grandma Fa's words. "There's a first time for everything," she said.

Some of the villagers agreed to join Mulan. They were excited to try something new!

Mulan and her teammates painted their boat to match Mushu's fiery red scales and orange belly.

"It does sort of look like me," Mushu said. "If not quite as handsome."

Training began the next day. The team needed a drummer to keep the beat for the rowers, so Mushu volunteered.

"I've had a lot of practice with banging a gong all these years," he said.

Mushu began drumming
a wild, uneven beat.

Paddles clashed!
The boat rocked!

One rower fell
into the water!

After the crew pulled their teammate back into the boat, Mulan showed Mushu how to keep a steady rhythm for the rowers to follow. She clapped her hands. *One, two, three.*

Listening to the beat, the team arced their paddles through the air. Soon they were paddling in unison!

Mulan was the team's sweep. It was her job to steer with a long oar.

At first, the boat zigged and zagged. Then the rowers heard Mushu's steady BAM, BAM, BAM.

They followed the beat and glided easily through the water.

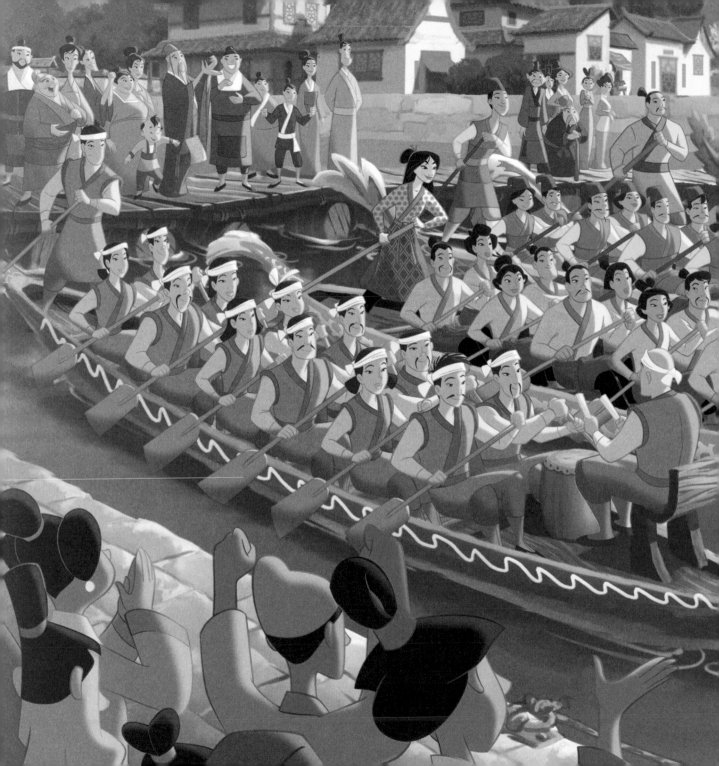

After weeks of practice, it was finally the day of the race. Mulan and
her team lined up their boat with the others, eager to start.

To "wake up" each dragon, red dots were painted onto the eyes.

The race began! The dragon boats zoomed away from shore, each drummer pounding out a different rhythm.

As the other boats whizzed past, Mulan's team struggled to hear Mushu's steady beat.

Mulan tried to steer as the waves from the other teams slapped against the sides of their boat. She clutched her oar as the boat tipped this way and that.

The drum bounced out of Mushu's hands and into the water!

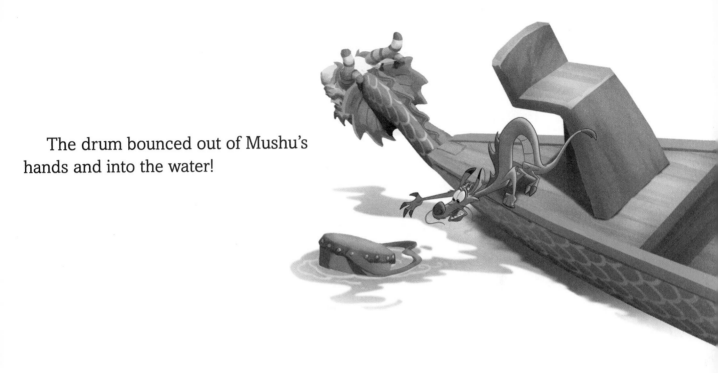

He reached out to grab it, and . . .

SPLASH!

Mulan fished Mushu out of the water. But without her steering, the boat crashed into the reeds!

Mulan's team slumped in their seats. How could they finish the race without a drum?

"We can't give up," Mulan told her teammates. "It's true that we've never paddled without a drum, but there's a first time for everything. Together, we can get to the finish line!"

"And I can still give you a steady beat!" Mushu said.
He clapped his hands.

CLAP,

CLAP,

CLAP.

The rowers smiled and lined up their paddles, ready to go.

Mulan and her teammates steered the boat back onto the river. The rowers paddled through the water to Mushu's beat, again and again, until they reached the finish line.

The crowd onshore greeted Mulan's team with cheers!
Although they were the last dragon boat to finish, they
were the first to complete the race without a drum.

That night, the village threw a party for Mulan and her team. They had tried something new and they hadn't given up—and that was worth celebrating!

Suddenly, a young performer ran up to Carine. "I did it," she said. "I sang out loud!"

"I heard you," said Carine. "Your voice was as sweet as a songbird's."

Princess Cinderella smiled. It warmed her heart to hear the very words she'd spoken to Carine all those years ago!

Now, years later, at the Royal Theater, Princess Cinderella
hugged Carine after the show.

"Your voice is as sweet as ever," she said.

"Thank you," Carine said. "I couldn't have done it without you, Princess."

"I have found a most talented student," Madame LaVoix
announced. "I predict Carine will be a great star one day!"
Everyone applauded—except Drizella and Anastasia.

Cinderella called out to the opera star. "Madame LaVoix! If you please, Carine would like to sing for you," she said.

Carine stood right in front of Madame LaVoix and sang in a voice that was as sweet as a songbird's.

Later, as Madame LaVoix headed for her carriage, Carine told Cinderella what had happened.

"It's not too late," Cinderella said. "If you believe in yourself, you can do anything."

Carine gave Cinderella a hug. "I think I'm ready to sing now."

But when Madame LaVoix arrived, Lady Tremaine sent Cinderella to do chores.

When it was Carine's turn to audition, she opened her mouth— and nothing came out!

Drizella and Anastasia were next. They sang a dreadful off-key duet.

Cinderella ran up to Carine. "I'll be right by your side for the audition," she told her. "Just be yourself. Remember, your voice is as sweet as a songbird's."

"Thank you," said Carine. "You know, I really do think I have a chance!"

At the next salon, Lady Tremaine made an announcement: "Madame LaVoix, a famous opera singer, is visiting tomorrow." She would select one student to study with her. It was the chance of a lifetime!

At the bakery, Carine sang louder. The baker clapped!

At the perfumery, Carine's voice was strong and full of energy. "Superb," cooed a patron.

First, Cinderella had Carine sing for the shopkeeper at the music store. Carine, feeling shy, sang softly for him. He thought she was charming.

At the blacksmith's, Carine sang more confidently. The blacksmith cheered.

The next day, Carine and Cinderella arrived in the town square. Cinderella had a plan to help Carine feel better about her singing.

It was time for Carine to see for herself how good she really was!

"Maybe they're right," Carine said to Cinderella
after the salon. "Maybe I should quit singing."

"I don't think so," said Cinderella. "I have an idea.
Meet me in town tomorrow."

"If you were smart," Drizella said, "you'd give up on singing."
"Just look at her. You can tell she's not special," Anastasia snarled.

When the salon began later that day, Anastasia and
Drizella continued to tease Carine.

The next day, Cinderella saw Carine in town.

"You sing beautifully," Cinderella said.

"Do you really think so?" asked Carine. "Anastasia said I sounded like a goose."

"That's not true!" Cinderella exclaimed. "Your voice is as sweet as a songbird's."

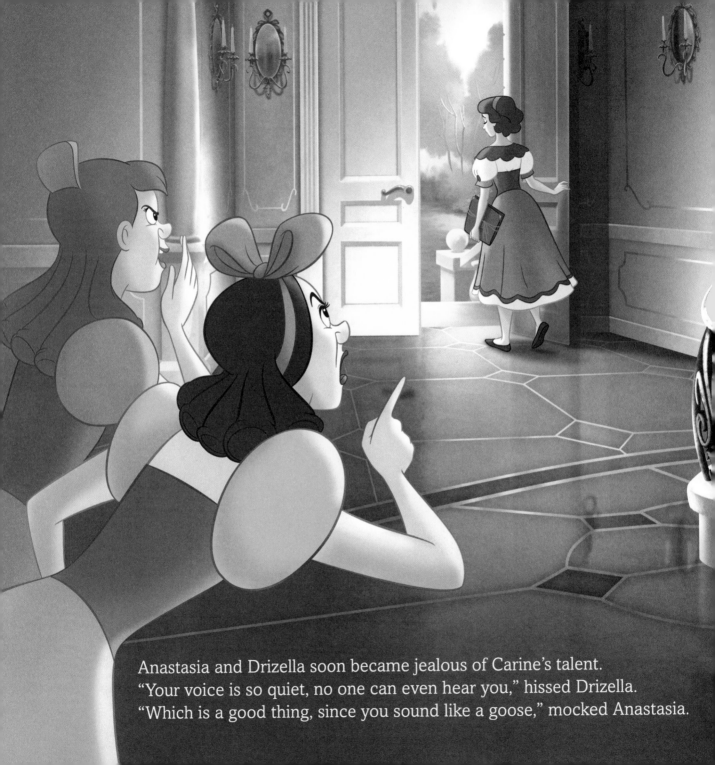

Anastasia and Drizella soon became jealous of Carine's talent.
"Your voice is so quiet, no one can even hear you," hissed Drizella.
"Which is a good thing, since you sound like a goose," mocked Anastasia.

Lady Tremaine's salon began the next day. Cinderella slipped away from her chores to peek in on the lessons. One girl caught her attention. She had the sweetest voice that Cinderella had ever heard!

The salon sounded boring to Lady Tremaine's two daughters, Drizella and Anastasia. But Cinderella wanted to attend.

Lady Tremaine said no. "You have far too many chores to do," she told her stepdaughter.

Years earlier, Cinderella's stepmother, Lady Tremaine, had decided
to host a salon at her chateau. It was a regular gathering where girls
could learn how to play an instrument and take singing lessons. And
it would make Lady Tremaine feel important.

It was opening night at the Royal Theater, and Princess Cinderella was excited to see the show. As the curtain went up, the star stepped onto the stage.

Cinderella smiled. It was Carine, a singer she had met long before she became a princess. . . .